I Sure Am Glad To See You,
BLACKBOARD BEAR

Martha Alexander

CANDLEWICK PRESS
CAMBRIDGE, MASSACHUSETTS

For Sean M.S.

Second edition 2001

Library of Congress Cataloging-in-Publication Data

Alexander, Martha G.
I sure am glad to see you, Blackboard Bear / Martha Alexander—2nd ed.
p.   cm.
Summary: Little Anthony's bear is immensely helpful when he has to deal with other
children who are teasing, selfish, or bullying.
ISBN 0-7636-0669-3
[1. Interpersonal relations—Fiction. 2. Sharing—Fiction. 3. Bears—Fiction.] I. Title.
PZ7.A3777   Iaam 2001
[E]—dc21   00-029754

2 4 6 8 10 9 7 5 3 1

Printed in Hong Kong

This book was typeset in Stempel Schneidler Roman.
The illustrations were done in colored pencil and watercolor.

Candlewick Press
2067 Massachusetts Avenue
Cambridge, Massachusetts 02140

Gloria, you have more toys than anyone in the world. Can I play with them?

Sure. Except for that one. It's brand new!

And not that one. It's my favorite.
But you can play with this whole box of things.

This is just a box of JUNK. You're selfish.
I'm not playing with you anymore.

Who cares!

I'm going to get a double ice-cream cone.

You'll be sorry, Gloria!

Help! Help! An alligator!

We fooled you! It isn't real!

That wasn't funny.
Just wait—you'll be sorry.

Hey, you! Give me back my ice cream!

Who's going to make me—you or your bear?

You're no help.

Oh, boy, I sure am glad to see *you*!

Things have been terrible around here.
That mean Stewart just took my ice cream.

I'll show *him*. I'll get another one.

I've got *you* for protection.

Wait here. I'll get your favorite for you—blueberry!

Hey, Anthony, you're a good kid!
You got me another ice cream too.

I did not! That's for my friend. Give it back!

Who's going to make me?

Here. Take it! Take it! You win.

What about my double ice cream you ate?

Listen, Anthony, I'll buy you a triple when
I get my allowance—I promise.

Well, all right, Stewart.
My bear feels *sure* you won't forget.

Scaredy-cat Stewart isn't so tough after all.

Hi, Anthony—what a beautiful bear!
Please, please be my friend—we could *share*.

All right, Gloria, I'll play with you—and Joe
and Julie too—and share *everything* . . .

except . . . of course . . . my bear!